The Three Little Pigs

Illustrated by Eileen Grace

Library of Congress Cataloging-in-Publication Data

Three little pigs.
   The three little pigs.

   SUMMARY: The third pig not only has a brick
house, but he is cleverer than his unfortunate
fellow pigs.
   [1. Folklore.   2. Pigs—Fiction]   I. Grace, Eileen.
PZ8.1.T383   1981   398.2'4529734   80-27483
ISBN 0-89375-462-5
ISBN 0-8167-5281-8 (pbk.)

This edition published in 2002.

Printed in the United States of America.

20 19 18 17 16 15 14 13 12

THE THREE LITTLE PIGS

Once upon a time, there were three little pigs. Their mother could not keep them, so she sent them out to seek their fortunes.

The first little pig met a man who had a bundle of straw. "Will you give me some of that straw?" asked the pig. The man gave him some straw, and the little pig set to work building a house.

He was finished in no time at all.

Before long, the wolf was at the door. He called out, "Little pig, little pig, let me come in!"

But the little pig answered, "No, not by the hair of my chinny chin chin!"

"Then I'll huff, and I'll puff, and I'll blow your house
in!" cried the wolf. Then he huffed, and he puffed, and
he blew the house in. And he ate up the little pig.

The second little pig met a man who had a bundle of sticks. "Will you give me some of those sticks?" asked the pig. The man gave him some sticks, and the little pig set to work building a house. He was finished in a very short time.

Before long, the wolf came along. He knocked at the door and called, "Little pig, little pig, let me come in!"

But the little pig answered, "No, not by the hair of my chinny chin chin!"

"Then I'll huff, and I'll puff, and I'll blow your house in!" cried the wolf. Then he huffed, and he puffed, and he puffed, and he huffed. He blew the house in, and he ate up the second little pig.

The third little pig met a man with a load of bricks. "Will you give me some of those bricks?" asked the pig. The man gave him some bricks, and the pig set to work building a house. It took a long time, but finally, he was finished.

Then along came the wolf. He knocked on the door and said, "Little pig, little pig, let me come in!"

But the little pig answered, "No, not by the hair of my chinny chin chin!"

"Then I'll huff, and I'll puff, and I'll blow your house in!" cried the wolf. So he huffed, and he puffed, and he puffed, and he huffed. Then he huffed, and he puffed some more. But he could *not* blow the house in.

Then the wolf thought of another idea. "Little pig, little pig," he called. "I know where there are some delicious turnips."

"Where?" asked the little pig.

"Not far from here, in a farmer's field," replied the wolf. "If you will be ready tomorrow morning at six o'clock, I will show you where they are."

"All right," agreed the pig. But he got up at five o'clock the next morning and went to find the turnips by himself.

At six o'clock, the wolf knocked on the pig's door. "Are you ready?" he called.

"Am I ready?" laughed the little pig. "I have already been there and back! Now I have all the turnips I can use."

So the wolf thought up a different plan. "Little pig, little pig," he called. "I know of an apple tree that is loaded with apples."

"Which one do you mean?" asked the little pig.

And the wolf replied, "It is far down the road. If you will be ready at five o'clock tomorrow morning, I will show you where it is."

The pig got up at four o'clock the next morning and found the apples by himself. But he was still up in the tree when the wolf arrived.

"So there you are!" called the wolf. "Why didn't you wait for me?"

The little pig called down, "I have been saving the best apples for you! Here, I will throw one down." But he threw it so far that the wolf had to chase after it. Then the little pig jumped down from the tree and ran all the way home with a sack full of apples.

The next morning, the wolf knocked on the little pig's door. "Little pig, little pig!" he called. "There is a fair in town. Would you care to go there with me?"

And the pig replied, "Yes, of course. What time will you be ready?"

"At three o'clock this afternoon," said the wolf.

"I will be ready for you," replied the little pig. Then, as soon as the wolf had gone home, the little pig went down to the fair by himself.

He bought a butter churn and was on his way home when he saw the wolf coming. So he climbed into the butter churn and rolled down the hill toward the wolf. This frightened the wolf so much that he ran all the way home.

The next day, the wolf knocked on the little pig's door and said, "Yesterday while I was walking to the fair, a great round thing came rumbling and tumbling down at me. It frightened me quite out of my wits!"

The little pig laughed, "Then you were frightened by me! You see, I went to the fair and bought a butter churn. When I saw you coming, I climbed into the churn and rolled down the hill."

This made the wolf so angry that he said he would come down the chimney and eat up the pig. Then he got a ladder and climbed up on the roof.

Meanwhile, the little pig built a big fire in the fireplace. He hung a huge pot of water over the fire. Before long, the water was boiling and bubbling.

The wolf came down the chimney and fell right into the pot! Then the little pig put the cover on and made a delicious stew, which he had for supper that very night!

And, of course, he lived happily ever after.